Slanted Windows

No Frills
<<<>>>
Buffalo
Buffalo, NY

Printed in the United States of America

Norris, Marjorie

Slanted Windows/Norris- 1st Edition

ISBN: 978-0989622097

1. Slanted Windows– Poetry 2. New Author – No Frills
Buffalo. 3. Poetry.
1. Title

No Frills Buffalo Press
119 Dorchester
Buffalo, New York 14213
For more information visit
Nofrillsbuffalo.com

Slanted Windows

by Marjorie Norris

<<<>>>

I am the heart of a murdered woman who took the wrong way home

--Margaret Atwood – "Owl Song",
from <u>You are Happy</u>,
(New York, New York: Harper and Row, 1974)

Heart

I am the heart of a murdered woman/
Who took the wrong way home.

I am a clerk at an office of law.
I file and file, everything
Alphabetical, my nails
Down to their quick,
My heart stamped even lower

I stand by my cabinet
Talking of codicils
(which are deadly)
Only 27, I die
At the hands
Of my payers

I offer myself
To the needs of bosses
And clients
As Siddhartha said,

They feed off me

Divorces and Marriages

I've seen them come and go,
Nudging me in the in back
Of my knees with their power,
Their devotion or freedom
At last

Cocktails

At the boss's party
I wear black and feathers—
I swoop from punch bowl
To champagne glass
Charming the best
Of them, empty
By the end of evening

Later

At home I make eggs and toast
Watch one channel on the television,
Brand new in this '50's apartment.
I watch John Cameron Swayze,
Say my prayers. My parents
Are gone and my sister Ida
Lives faraway in Moab

I miss her and my nieces
But daily this is my life,
Alphabetizing at the law
Offices all their needs

Why Why

How I became submerged
In this dim lost corridor
I do not know: I've had
So few options, no college,
No ability to become
A nurse or teacher, few
Chances to meet
Future mates

Feline

My cat sustains me
Jewel as marmalade
Orange as dawn

Let poached eggs
And dry toast
Not deceive you—
They are a king's meal,
Munched near the slanted
Windows of my parlor
Or daily near
The jalousies
In the boss's office

A Day Off

I take a day from the office
To buy new shoes, penny loafers
For my aching feet
A movie for my aching heart

Later, Marmalade winds
Her tail in and out my legs
In the garden
As I weed the coreopsis
And the daisies

I know I need to find
A friend—not one
In a book or dream,
But one in life

I am so lonely
And unattended to:
I need to feed someone
Feed myself

The Busy Day

Mr. Brewster, my boss,
Comes up behind my desk
Places his hands
On my tight shoulders,
Did you have a good
Day off?   he purrs,
And I tremble as I reach
For my pencil, a silent
Offering to his
Dictation

Book Club

There's a readers' group
Beginning at the library,
No more than six,
And we can share
The classics. Today
At last I meet a friend
Her name is Patricia,
She has a dog,
Not a cat, but she
Works in an office
Not far from mine:
Import/Export
She says, and
For the first time
In many months
I laugh

Patricia

The day I met Patricia
Was the day I began
To know the city:
She took me to gallery
Openings, and plays
Where actors read,
Most were free
Or admittance a small
Donation: I felt
That I had known
This life always,
The sidewalks,
The L-Train,
The little ferries
That buoyed
An inner life

Situational

The war had been over for about six years
And I knew that jobs were slim,
Mr. Brewster came to my office
Pressed his pudgy fingers
Against his fuzzy temples,
His gold signet ring
Pointed toward me,
The diamond chiseled,
Cutting

I need you to leave here,
He said sadly, you've
Been a good employee,
Compliant, quiet, cowed:
You are what I esteem
Most

But I must let you go now
Let you go

Terror

I lived in quiet terror the first few days
Had my phone cut off to save cash
Couldn't afford even a party line
Heard from no one

Then Patricia appeared at the door,
Carrying a fern, a smile on her face
What? Now, now, she mused,

You must live with me

What fun we will have,
Cooking, shopping, sharing
Clothes

You can do my errands,
And I will do yours

You will find another job
Another job for sure

Quickening

My Irish grandmother told me
How to save a nicke., I mused
As Patricia and I scoured
The markets, and bought
Vegetables cheaply
Making stews

Movies and galleries were
Very plentiful

And soon I found two
Jobs: one at the Rialto
And another at
The Plumed Serpent,
A modern gallery
Close by

Hope

Patricia always had that hope in her
She'd invested in it early,
Having come from poverty
And a wild throng of children

She gave it to me and I gladly
Grabbed it up, hope, the wild throng,
The story of overcoming
All the little adversities

Food

This is a feast:
My days at the gallery,
Listening to each pedantic
Or vibrant witness
Of viewers and observers,
These paintings, sculptures
With their own lessons

And I am here
To learn their truths,
Abstract, impressionistic
Or post-impressionist,
Landscape or pastoral,

This is the heart
Where I reside,
Sinew, breath, and bone,
These are my feet,
The ground I grow in

Later

Later at night
At the cinema,
The students and professors
Line up for replays of *Adam's Rib*
And *Blood and Sand*. I watch
Their dark eyes as they pass
Money to me for a ticket
Their eyes widening with the promise
Of story and escape

Floating

I feel that I am a vessel
On the path to some
Unknown promise—
And they, these people
And the movies,
Are instruments
For my own change

And yes. I do know
This. I am changing!
I can feel this
At the Rialto
As I clip on each
Circular whirring reel

Life

My life is happier:
Now I sense the joys
I experience as Pat
And I tour this city:
Now life's mysteries
Come like flowers,
Jasmine, red lily
In evening's shade
In our apartment,
Just after the muted
Nape of dusk

Dawn

From my burnished bedroom window,
After the canary flies out of wheat fields
Towards smoky morn, mysteries
Shriek like hawks that circle
Messianic just up over
The hills, whose selves
Open like boxes, nesting,
Pandora, me, or
The whirlwind

Patience

Patience is waiting for your hormones
To catch up with your mind
And both of you catching the L-train
To South Chicago, spilling graffiti
Like carnage, no small insult,
To write your will upon the land
Or school or factory building

Patience 2

Patience is watching your sister's children
Grow when you are not sure you are at all,
Scrubbing counters, floors, your soul
Like dysentery and you, mopping up

Patience 3

Patior, the root word, Latin,
To suffer through, overcome
To put some feeling
On the shelf, to keep
Your heat down
To a dull roar
In the night,
The sheets up
Under your chin
While you gaze out
At the chill moon,
Frozen stars spilling
Over a crunch of snow

Textile

Where is the factory where the shop girls spin?
It's in the textile district where hearts
Are sewn and treasured, tied up
Under the closed purview of bosses
With veined temples throbbing

It's in the heart of a universe
Where women gather: sewing, working.
Machines rattling, humming

Queue

I ask them to form
A line, tell them
I'll gather inks
And paints to put
Upon their muslin

Each takes a piece
As large as a bed-
Sheet: the office girls
And factory girls
Unite, organizing,
Forming a union
Of labor and needs,
A line of public
Sentiment, slogans,
"Together or bust"

Like prayer-cloths
On the street,
Catching the air

In the Night

Waiting for dawn
As I sit here
Typing

Flyers for the workers

Their union

Not mine

I'm still in the shop
At the gallery

My life is far
From secure

But how I love it anyway

And now to have those
Workers love their lot!

Though now paint
Must be scraped from factory
Windows for light

And angora flies
In the air
Like cottonwood

And women
Inhale brown lung

Small Moments

Two hurricane lamps splash red light
On the spare table
Lamps, please light my way

The difference between us matters,
Each slippered step
The way you pour tea

My old cat had a yin-yang face,
White long-sprung whiskers:
She grooms herself now

At ninety-four, my grandmother
Cannot hear, I repeat all messages
Again, again

But someone watches, knows
Each person, each frail power
Each earthquake as it rumbles

I do know the stroke
Of a pen, the brush
Of pine near
The skirted path

Rally

I bring them all together:
The artists, they are poor
(and the poor have always
been with us)

they need apartments
they can afford, clean,
no rats or roaches,
just the way light
slants on autumn
afternoons, the dancing
of a sunbeam though
the motes of dust

and the office workers
and the women who do
textiles, they
are all shrouded
in the garments
of history

once I was an office worker
who had no power,
just the limits of my own
little cubicle, but then
hope burst out,
I was never "cowed"
as my employer
said when he
fired me

Patricia

She's led me here:
Her optimism and joy,
Her intuitive faith in me,
How I have come
To love her—the way
Her auburn hair
Falls in small curls
At her neck,
The erotics
Of our life together

One Day

Along Lake Michigan's edge
One day, I felt the whirlpool
Both me and water

They were my life,
The water and the land,
The artists and their lofts
The factories and apartments

Then one day I looked up,
Patricia, and there you stood,
Smiling, halo'd, sure.
With brown bright eyes:
They skipped the water
Like stone

About the Author

Marjorie Norris has published poems in *Wide Open*, *Jugglers' World*, *Arizona Mandala*, *Poets Against Apartheid*, *Room of Our Own Buffalo News*, *Beyond Bones*, *Translation of Silence*, *Santa Rosa Review*, *Rain and Thunder*, *The Other Herald*, *Artvoice*, *Persimmon Tree*, *Words over Easy*, and *Brigid's Fire*, *Earth's Daughters* and *A Celebration of Western New York Poets*.

She has won Just Buffalo's Writer in Residence award for poetry, and an honorable mention in Greensboro, NC Triad award, also teaching at Womonwrites in Atlanta, Feminist Writers in Ithaca, State University at Buffalo's Women's Studies Poetry Project and Just Buffalo's Writers-In-Education. She received two New York State Council on the Arts grants to explore writing with those living with HIV, included in the anthology Full Circle. Marjorie Norris has taught creative writing at Chautauqua Institution Special Studies Program in Writing and did a workshop for the Roycroft Wordsmiths.

Her books include *Chautauqua Breathing*, *Two Suns*, *Two Moons*, *Resilience*, and *Woodland Heart*, including an anthology called *Trees of Surprise*, about an October storm in 2007.

Acknowledgements

The author would like to thank the Monday-morning writers at Allen Street's Café 59, Women of the Crooked Circle, also Colleen Gannon, Kathleen Betsko Yale, Frederick E. Whitehead, and Tim Maggio.

www.ingramcontent.com/pod-product-compliance
Lightning Source LLC
Chambersburg PA
CBHW061504170626
46811CB00004B/1604